8 · 8 · 18

This book

D0591014

Contents

First published 2011 by Brown Watson
The Old Mill, 76 Fleckney Road,
Kibworth Beauchamp, Leic LE8 0HG

ISBN: 978-0-7097-1931-1

My Little Book of

Farm Stories

Illustrations by Gill Guile

Brown Watson

ENGLAND

An Exciting Surprise!

Farmer Jones has exciting news
when he opens the mail.
"Wow!" he shouts, waking up Mrs Jones, who is
dozing off after milking the cows so early.
"I have won that Dairy Show prize
– a brand new tractor!"

He waves his sausage about, rattling the
cups as he leaps up, yelling, "Yippee!"

The new tractor arrives the very next day.

"Isn't she incredible?" laughs Farmer Jones.

Goat and Duck stare in
amazement as he sings loudly:
"Oh, beautiful tractor, you are mine,
How you glitter; how you shine
Now round the farm let's ride and climb."

Farmer Jones grins from ear to ear. He keeps
stopping and getting out so that he can look
at the tractor properly again and pat
her shiny red paint.

"It is almost dark now!" hoots Owl.

Mrs Jones goes to bed ready to rise early
again next morning at milking time but Farmer
Jones is still driving around singing:
"Even the stars don't shine as bright
As my new tractor does tonight."

He is the happiest farmer in the world!

Daisy Wants a Friend

Daisy Duckling is lonely. She was the first egg
to hatch and the other eggs show no signs of
cracking yet. So Daisy sets off through the
reeds to see if she can find a friend who
wants to play on the stream or riverbank.

Soon Daisy meets a beautiful snowy
swan with two baby cygnets.

"Will you play with me?" asks Daisy.

"Not today," cheep the cygnets. "We are just
off to visit Great Grandma Swan. She is going
to give us gliding lessons."

So little Daisy paddles on further down the river.

Next Daisy meets Mrs Turkey
and her three baby poults.

"Will you play with me?" asks Daisy.

"Not today," cheep the poults.
"We are just off to visit Grandpa Turkey.
He is going to teach us how to gobble-gobble!"

Sad, lonely Daisy waddles back home again.

"Where have you been?" asks her mother.
"Look, I have a wonderful surprise for you."

The other eggs have hatched at last.
So now three little ducklings have joined
the family: "Quack! Quack! Quack!"

Daisy has two brothers and a sister to play
with her now. She will never be lonely again.

Gregory Goat is Puzzled

Gregory Goat is puzzled. His lamb friends have just had their first haircut and look very strange with all their woolly hair sheared away.

"I don't know who's who any more," sighs Gregory. "Shelley had brambles under her chin; Joe had mud on his tummy and Sheila had big curls."

"Don't worry, Gregory," says Bluebird,
"I know them all by their different baas
and their voices have not been sheared
away so let me introduce you."

"Baa," laughs Shelley.
"Baa-aagh!" sighs Joe.
"Baar-behhhrr-baaaar," bleats Sheila.

"Hello again, friends," says Gregory,
grinning happily.

Chilly Chicks

One snowy day, Mrs Hen says to her chicks,
"I must go and fetch some fresh straw for our
beds to keep us warm and snug tonight. Stay
here and play nicely until I am back."

Philly, Dilly and Lilly have great fun throwing
snowballs but after a while they begin to shiver.

Mrs Hen seems to have been gone
such a long time. "Let's see if we can
find her," Philly suggests.

"Have you seen our mum?"
Dilly asks kind Katy Cow.
"No, I'm sorry," moos Katy, her sweet
warm breath gusting over the chicks,
"I don't know where she is."

"Have you seen our mum?"
Lilly asks Gloria Goose.
"No, I'm sorry," replies Gloria, wrapping
her fluffy warm wing around
the three shivering chicks,
"I don't know where she is. Honk! Honk!"

Suddenly there is a loud "Cluck! Cluck!"
behind them and they all jump.

"So, there you are!" cries a cross Mrs Hen.
"I was so worried when I couldn't find
you back home."

"Your babies are quite safe," says Gloria.
"Right, off you go, rascals.
And do as you are told next time."
"We will," cheep the chicks
but they probably won't!

Best Friends

The rabbits love Old Scarecrow Bill
And dance around and play
As Bill sings a merry song or two
And laughs loudly every day.
Bill tells how Farmer Fred says,
"Here's a coat, best friend, for you;
And have this jolly, tall top hat
And gloves of brightest blue."

Young Fred always comes to see him,
Every single day ...
He drives his tractor up and down
As the sheep all baa and say,
"Here comes young Farmer Fred again
To see Old Scarecrow Bill,"
As the puffing tractor pants and chugs
And scrambles up the hill.

Paws Pup Dreams

Paws, the farm puppy, is having a nightmare. "Wuff! Wuff!" barks Paws, suddenly waking up, as he growls and leaps into the air, sending his bowl flying.

"Oh, thank goodness. I am here safe in my basket, after all," he pants. "What a relief!"

Paws follows the farmer outside
and talks to the hens.
"What is your best dream?" he asks.
"That I lay a golden egg," clucks Jenny Hen.
"That my chicks are little angels and do as they
are told for once," clucks Penny Hen as all the
farm animals gather around to listen.

"What do you like to dream about most?"
Paws asks them.

"Cool ponds and shiny fish," quacks Duck.
"Sweet new grass," baas Sheep.
"Black crows and golden buttercups,"
laughs Scarecrow.
"Warm sunshine and lily pads," croaks Frog.
"Lettuce," giggles Rabbit.
"A new bonnet," sighs Goose, "with ribbons."

This conversation makes Paws sleepy
so he patters back inside.

"My best dream," he wuffs contentedly as he
rolls and wriggles on his rug, "is a HUGE supper,
a new, chewy bone and a warm, cosy bed.
Aaaah-wuff-zzzzzz!" Soon he is fast asleep
and dreaming of chasing cats.

Birthday Surprise

"Oh, my goodness! Oh dear, dear! How could
I forget?" clucks Henny Penny, rushing out to
find her chicks, "I need your help! All of you!
Quickly!" she cries. "Today is Mrs Moo's birthday
and everyone has forgotten about it.
We need to make a cake – straight away!
Oh dear, dear, dear!"

Soon everyone in the farm is busy.
The chicks slice a tasty pie to share out.
Henny Penny ices a wonderful cake.
The turkeys make gobble-gobble sandwiches
and all the animals wrap presents. Then,
together, they race across the meadow,
singing "Happy Birthday" as they go.

Mrs Moo is snoozing. She, too, has
completely forgotten her birthday. She wakes
up and looks in amazement at the presents,
cake and slices of pie. Then she moos, "How
kind you all are. I am so happy I forgot
as it makes this surprise even more surprising!
Thank you sooooo much. Mooooo!"

Fun Farm Times

Sally and Simon live on a farm
And are busy all year long:
They help to feed the hens
And to drive the cows along;
They cuddle lonely lambs
And sing the kittens songs.

They have to go to school, of course,
But they run home every day,
Ready to see the cows milked
And to give the horses hay;
But leaving time to kick a ball about
And to watch the rabbits play.